HIND POCKET BOOKS

The pleasures of VEGETARIAN COOKERY

The pleasures of VEGETARIAN COOKERY

JASLEEN DUGGAL

HIND POCKET BOOKS
An imprint of Penguin Random House

HIND POCKET BOOKS

USA | Canada | UK | Ireland | Australia
New Zealand | India | South Africa | China | Singapore

Hind Pocket Books is part of the Penguin Random House group of companies whose addresses can be found at www.hindpocketbooks.com

Published by Penguin Random House India Pvt. Ltd
4th Floor, Capital Tower 1, MG Road,
Gurugram 122 002, Haryana, India

Penguin Random House India

First published in Hind Pocket Books by Penguin Random House India 2019"
This edition published in 2022

10 9 8 7 6 5 4 3 2

ISBN 9789353493837

Printed at Repro India Limited

www.penguin.co.in

FSC www.fsc.org MIX Paper from responsible sources FSC® C047271

This is a legitimate digitally printed version of the book and therefore might not have certain extra finishing on the cover.

Contents

Soups

Dals

Vegetables

Rice and Breads

Curd Recipes

Desserts and Indian Sweets

Snacks and Soft Drinks

Chutneys, Sauces and Pickles

Cookery Terms and Their Meanings

Batter : A mixture of gram flour, water, salt, garam masala etc. It is left for sometime to swell.

Blanch : To boil in boiling water in order to remove the skin.

Blend : To mix two or more ingredients thoroughly.

Chop : To cut into small pieces.

Coating consistency : When a thin coating appears on the back of a spoon after it is dipped in a mixture and removed.

Croutons : Bread trimmed of crusts cut to shape and sauted in oil or butter.

Cut in : To combine fat and dry ingredients with two knives as when making pastry.

Dice : To cut into very small cubes e.g., carrots or cottage cheese.

Dough : A mixture of flour and water kneaded till it is smooth and not sticky.

Fold in : To mix the ingredients lightly.

Parboiled : Half cooked or partially cooked.

Puree : Pulp of cooked fruit or vegetable obtained through a seive.

Saute : To fry lightly in a small amount of fat.

Simmer : To cook in a liquid with heat sufficient to keep it just below boiling point.

Weights and Measures

As far as weights and measures are concerned, the use of cups and spoons has been made in order to simplify the recipe.

	1 cup	1 tbsp
Pulses		
Bengal gram	150 gms	
Bengal gram flour	90 gms	
Dry beans	165 gms	
Kabuli chana	150 gms	
Rajmah	150 gms	
Cereals		
Cornflour	90 gms	10 gms
Flour (maida)	110 gms	10 gms
Rice	170 gms	20 gms
Wheat flour	110 gms	
Fluids		
Milk or water	180 ml	20 ml
Curd	180 gms	30 gms
Milk ½ litre	1 bottle	
Cream	200 gms	20 gms
Fats & oils		
Ghee (melted)	150 gms	12 gms
Ghee unmelted oil	180 gms	20 gms
Butter	170 gms	20 gms
Dry Fruits		
Groundnuts (shelled)	120 gms	15 gms
Raisins	120 gms	20 gms
Walnuts (shelled)	120 gms	
Miscellaneous		
Khoya	110 gms	15 gms
Cheese (mashed)	125 gms	
Sugar	190 gms	20 gms
Jaggery	200 gms	20 gms

OVEN TEMPERATURE

The recipes state whether the oven should be slow, moderate, hot or very hot, and give the indicative temperature in degrees. °Centigrade as a guide. The actual instructions of the manufacturer should be referred to for further guidance, and adjustments made according to your own experience and results.

	°F	°C	Gas Mark
Very Cool	250°F =	121°C	1/4
	275°F =	135°C	1/2
Cool	300°F =	149°C	1, 2
Warm	325°F =	163°C	3
Moderate	350°F =	177°C	4
Fairly Hot	375°F =	191°C	5
	400°F =	204°C	6
Hot	425°F =	218°C	7
Very Hot	450°F =	232°C	8
	475°F =	246°C	9

To convert Fahrenheit into Centigrade: Subtract 32, multiply by 5, then divide by 9. To convert Centigrade into Fahrenheit: multiply by 9, divide by 5, then 32.

SYMBOLS USED

teaspoon	tsp	grams	gm
tablespoon	tbsp	litre	ltr
kilograms	kg	millilitre	ml
minutes	mins.		

Soups

Soups are a meal in themselves. A variety of soups with exciting flavours can be made from any vegetable stock.

Soups may be light and clear or thick and hearty dishes. Garnishes are important – they can add tremendously to the look and taste of the soup and take only minutes to prepare. Chopped coriander and other fresh herbs, fried croutons of bread, a dollop of light sour cream – all add colour, texture and extra vitamins.

Croutons

Remove crusts from 6-8 slices of white bread and cut each slice into 4.

Brush both sides with oil – place in a single layer on a tray and bake in a slow oven at 150°C until crisp and golden. Alternatively croutons may be deep fried until golden brown and crisp.

TOMATO SOUP
TAMATAR KA SOUP

Serves : 6-8
Preparation Time : 10mins.
Cooking Time : 20 mins.

INGREDIENTS

Tomatoes 10 medium	Butter 1 tbsp
Ginger 2 cm piece	Milk 1 cup
Carrots 2 to 3	Water 5 cups
Cornflour 1 to 2 tbsp	Salt to taste

METHOD

1. Cut the tomatoes into small pieces, chop ginger and grate carrots.
2. Put them in a pressure cooker, add water, and pressure cook for 7 minutes.
3. Mash the vegetables and make a puree.
4. Heat butter in a pan, add cornflour, brown it lightly, take it off the stove and add milk.
5. Put it on the fire again, add the vegetable puree and let it simmer. Cook till it thickens, stirring constantly for 2-3 minutes.
6. Serve garnished with croutons.

Note: Croutons could be served with any soup.

Spinach Soup
Palak ka Soup

Serves : 6
Preparation Time : 15 mins.
Cooking Time : 40 mins.

Ingredients

- Spinach 500 gm
- Onion 1 medium
- Water 3 cups
- Milk 1 cup
- Cheese 50 gm
- Bread 2 slices
- Ghee or butter 1 tsp
- Sugar ¼ tsp
- Salt ½ tsp

Method

1. Wash, clean and chop the spinach leaves finely and chop the onion. Mash the bread slices well.
2. Melt ghee in a pan or cooker and fry onion till golden brown.
3. Add spinach, salt, sugar, mashed bread and water. Bring to boil and cook for half an hour or pressure cook it for 10 minutes.
4. Rub the mixture through a sieve.
5. Add milk and reheat the soup.
6. Serve hot topped with grated cheese in each cup.

Pea Soup
Matar ka Soup

Serves	:	12
Preparation Time	:	6 hrs.
Cooking Time	:	30 mins.

Ingredients

- Peas shelled 500 gm
- Water 2 ltr
- Onion chopped 1 large
- Milk ¼ pint
- Coriander leaves chopped a few
- Butter 1 tsp
- Pepper ¼ tsp
- Salt to taste

Method

1. Soak the green peas in cold water for about 5-6 hours.
2. Put the peas, onion, coriander leaves and butter in a pan with water, and boil until the peas are very tender.
3. Rub through a sieve, add milk, salt and pepper.
4. Boil it again just before serving.

CREAMED ONION SOUP
PYAZ KA SOUP MALAI KE SATH

Serves : 4
Preparation Time : 10 mins.
Cooking Time : 15 mins.

INGREDIENTS

Onions 4 large

Butter 50 gm

Cornflour 2 tbsp

Vegetable stock or water 2 cups

Cream ½ cup

Milk 1 cup

Salt and pepper to taste

METHOD

1. Slice onions.
2. Melt butter in a saucepan, fry onions till golden brown. Then add cornflour and cook for 1-2 minutes.
3. Remove the pan from the heat and gradually add water or stock and milk.
4. Bring to boil and cook until soup thickens.
5. Season with salt and pepper and mix the cream before serving.

Cream of Mushroom Soup
Guchchi ka Soup

Serves	:	6
Preparation Time	:	15 mins.
Cooking Time	:	15 mins.

Ingredients

- Fresh mushrooms 250 gm
- Water 3 cups
- Milk 1 cup
- Flour 2 tbsp
- Butter 2 tbsp
- Cream 3-4 tbsp
- Salt and pepper to taste

Method

1. Wash and chop mushrooms finely.
2. Melt butter in a pan, fry mushrooms for 2-3 minutes, stirring constantly.
3. Add the flour and cook for 1-2 minutes.
4. Remove the pan from the fire and gradually add water and milk.
5. Bring to boil and cook until it thickens.
6. Remove from the fire.
7. Season with salt and pepper and serve garnished with cream.

Dals

Dals or pulses are very rich in proteins and vitamins. Dals when sprouted are a good source of Vitamin C. They are easy to preserve in every kitchen and provide a good substitute when vegetables are not easily available. Dals can be cooked both as a substitute and in combination with vegetables. Dals can also be cooked in different ways.

Some precautions should always be taken while cooking dals.

1. *Do not cook the dal uncovered.*
2. *Try and pressure cook dal, as long cooking destroys its food value and colour.*
3. *Use all the water the dal was previously soaked in for the cooking.*
4. *To enhance the taste of dal, add fried onions with different spices and ghee.*
5. *While cooking, if there is need to add more water, always add boiling water.*

Sambar

Khatti Arhar Dal

Serves : 4-6
Preparation Time : 30 mins.
Cooking Time : 30 mins.

Ingredients

Arhar dal (split peas) 100 gm	Coconut, grated 1 tbsp
Potato 1 medium	Ghee 2 tbsp
Carrots 2 medium	Sambar masala 1 tsp
Brinjals 2 medium	Curry leaves 3-4
Turmeric powder 1 tsp	Mustard seeds 1 tsp
Tamarind pulp 4 tbsp	Green chillies 2
Cumin seeds ½ tsp	Water 4 cups
Coriander seeds 1 tsp	Salt 1 tsp

Method

1. Wash and soak the dal in water for half an hour.
2. Chop carrots, potato and brinjals.
3. Boil dal in the water in which it was soaked with carrot, potato, brinjals, salt, and turmeric till dal becomes tender, or pressure cook for 3-4 minutes.
4. Squeeze out the tamarind pulp and add to the boiled dal. Simmer for 10 minutes.
5. Heat the ghee in a frying pan and fry cumin and coriander seeds and grated coconut.
6. Remove them from the ghee and grind into a fine paste.

7. In the same ghee fry mustard seeds, finely cut green chillies and curry leaves.
8. Add the ground paste and cook for 5 minutes.
9. Then season dal with fried masala and sambar powder.
10. Serve hot with dosas or boiled rice.

Whole Moong Dal
Sabut Moong ki Dal

Serves : 4
Preparation Time : 30 mins.
Cooking Time : 20 mins.

Ingredients

Sabut moong dal 1 cup	Onion 1 small
Garlic ½ pod	Ghee 2 tbsp
Green chillies 3-4	Water 3 cups
Turmeric powder ½ tsp	Salt 1 tsp
Cumin seeds 2 tsp	

Method

1. Clean, wash and soak dal for half an hour.
2. Chop garlic and green chillies.
3. Put dal, water, garlic, green chillies, turmeric and salt in a pan.
4. Boil for 10 minutes with lid on the pan and keep cooking till required consistency is obtained.
5. Heat ghee, add sliced onion and cumin seeds.
6. Fry till onion is brown. Pour this into the dal. Serve hot.

Sour Bengal Gram

Khatta Kabuli Chana

Serves : 4
Preparation Time : Overnight
Cooking Time : 45 mins.

Ingredients

- Kabuli chana 1 cup
- Ginger 1 cm piece
- Onion 1 large
- Garlic 4 cloves
- Green chillies 1-2
- Tomato sliced 1 large
- Potatoes boiled and peeled 2 small
- Ghee 3 tbsp
- Coriander powder ½ tsp
- Turmeric powder ½ tsp
- Cumin seeds ½ tbsp
- Garam masala ½ tbsp
- Tamarind pulp 2 tbsp
- Water 3 cups
- Salt to taste

Method

1. Soak the chana overnight with a pinch of salt.
2. Chop and grind ginger, garlic and onion finely. Cut the potatoes in cubes.
3. Heat ghee and fry the potatoes lightly and keep them aside.
4. In the same ghee add onion, ginger and garlic paste and fry it till it becomes brown.
5. Add chopped green chillies, turmeric, coriander powder, cumin seeds and salt.
6. Cook for 2-3 minutes, then add chana and water.

7. Let it cook on slow fire. Cook till chana is tender and water dries up.
8. Add the tamarind pulp, and garam masala, mix it well.
9. Remove it from the fire. Serve garnished with potatoes and sliced tomato.

Black Bengal Gram — Dry

Sookha Kala Chana

Serves : 6
Preparation Time : Overnight
Cooking Time : 40 mins.

Ingredients

Chana 500 gm	Cumin seeds 1 tsp
Chopped onions 2 large	Coriander powder 1 tsp
Chopped tomatoes 3-4 medium	Garam masala 1 tbsp
Finely sliced garlic 6 flakes	Pomegranate seed powder 1 tsp
Finely sliced ginger 2-cm piece	Chilli powder and salt to taste
Turmeric powder ½ tbsp	Ghee 3 tbsp

Method

1. Soak chana overnight. To chana add turmeric powder and salt.
2. Pressure cook for 30 minutes or till tender and dry.
3. Grind cumin seeds after roasting to make cumin seed powder.
4. Heat ghee in a pan, fry chopped onions till golden brown. Then add sliced garlic and ginger and tomatoes.
5. Add boiled chana and mix well.
6. Season with ground cumin powder, coriander powder, garam masala, pomegranate seed powder and chilli powder. Cook for 5 minutes.
7. Serve hot.

White Bengal Gram
Kabuli Chana

Serves : 4
Preparation Time : Overnight
Cooking Time : 1 hr.

Ingredients

Kabuli chana 1 cup	Cumin powder ½ tsp
Soda-bicarbonate 1 pinch	Cardamom powder ½ tsp
Tea leaves 2 tsp	Sliced green chillies 2
Pomegranate seed powder 1 tsp	Onion 1 medium
Ghee ½ cup	Sliced lime 1
Coriander powder 1 tsp	Water 2 cups
Chilli powder 1 tsp	Salt 1½ tsp

Method

1. Pick and wash the chana. Soak overnight.
2. Boil chana in water with soda-bicarb, and tea leaves tied in a muslin cloth in a pressure cooker. Pressure cook for 40 minutes.
3. When steam has settled, open cooker, discard the stock and tea leaves.
4. Mix the dry masala with the chana and then cook again for about 2-3 minutes. Remove from the fire.
5. Heat ghee in a pan. When it is hot, pour it over the chana. Garnish with green chillies, onion sliced into rings and sliced lime.
6. Serve hot with bhaturas or puris.

Vegetables

In India we have a large variety of vegetables which provide all the nutrients that we need – starch, proteins, phosphates, carbohydrates, calcium, calories, etc. Cooking differs from person to person and region to region. There are a number of different ways in which vegetables can be prepared to cater to varied tastes.

A few points to be taken into consideration while cooking vegetables are:

1. *You need fresh vegetables to begin with. Wash vegetables thoroughly to free them from sand and dirt.*
2. *Cook vegetables just long enough to get them tender. Long cooking destroys the crispness and freshness of vegetables, as well as much of their food value and colour.*
3. *After washing do not let vegetables stand in water for a long time.*

4. *Vegetables should be boiled in as little water as possible. Do not put the vegetables in water until the water has started boiling, and remove them as soon as they are tender.*
5. *Save the water in which vegetables have been boiled or steamed (except potatoes) and use it for soups, gravies or sauces.*
6. *Green vegetables retain their colour better, if cooked uncovered for the first few minutes.*
7. *Stir vegetables only when you must. When you stir them, you destroy some of the vitamins.*

Cauliflower in Tomato Sauce
Phoolgobhi Mussalam

Serves : 4
Preparation Time : 10 mins.
Cooking Time : 30 mins.

Ingredients

Cauliflower 1 medium	Cumin seeds 2 tsp
Onions 2 small	Butter or ghee 2 tbsp
Garlic ½ pod	Lime juice 1 tbsp
Tomatoes 250 gm	Coriander leaves 1 sprig
Turmeric powder ½ tsp	Salt to taste
Green chillies 2	

Method

1. Remove the hard stem of cauliflower and wash.
2. Place the cauliflower with stem in a pressure cooker.
3. Add a little water and $^1/_2$ tsp of salt. Pressure cook it for 3-4 minutes. Blanch the tomatoes and remove the skins. Grind onions and garlic.
4. Fry the onions in butter till golden brown, add ground garlic, turmeric powder, chopped green chillies, cumin seeds and salt.
5. Cook for 1-2 minutes, add tomato pulp and cook for another 3-4 minutes. Remove it from the fire.
6. Arrange the cauliflower in a flat dish and pour the prepared tomato sauce over it. Bake in a moderately heated oven for about 5-7 minutes.
7. Serve hot sprinkled with lime juice and chopped coriander leaves.

Cauliflower in White Sauce
Phoolgobhi

Serves	:	4
Preparation Time	:	10 mins.
Cooking Time	:	15 mins.

Ingredients

Cauliflower 1 medium	Milk 1 cup
Tomatoes, sliced 2 small	Mustard powder 1 pinch
Potatoes, boiled & sliced 2 small	Grated cheese — Amul 4 tbsp
Flour 2 tbsp	Salt and pepper to taste
Butter 1 tbsp	

Method

1. Steam the cauliflower in a pressure cooker in half a cup of salted water for 2-3 minutes. Bring down the pressure immediately and drain the extra water in the cooker.

To make the white sauce –

Heat butter in a pan and add flour and cook lightly.

When light brown, add milk, salt and pepper. Keep stirring it continuously till it thickens. Add grated cheese and remove from the fire.

2. Arrange the cauliflower in a flat dish. Pour the sauce over the cauliflower.
3. Garnish with sliced tomatoes and potatoes.

MIXED VEGETABLE STEW
SABZION KA STEW

Serves : 4
Preparation Time : 15 mins.
Cooking Time : 10 mins.

INGREDIENTS

- Potatoes 6
- Onions 2
- Mint leaves ½ bunch
- Carrots 2
- French beans 10 to 12
- Tomatoes 3 medium
- Ghee 4 tsp
- Salt and pepper to taste

METHOD

1. Wash all the vegetables.
2. Peel potatoes, carrots and onions.
3. Chop onions, potatoes, carrots and French beans.
4. Blanch tomatoes, remove their skins and take out the pulp.
5. Chop the mint leaves.
6. Put all the vegetables and tomato pulp in a pan with one cup water, ghee, salt and pepper.
7. Steam for ten minutes.
8. Take the pan off the fire and serve hot.

Pea stew — South Indian Style
Matar Stew

Serves : 4
Preparation Time : 15 mins.
Cooking Time : 15 mins.

Ingredients

Fresh green peas 2 cups

Mint leaves 1 bunch

Butter 2 tbsp

Coconut, grated 1

Lime 1 tbspSugar 2 tsp

Salt to taste

Method

1. Shell and wash the peas.
2. Put the green peas, butter, and mint leaves in a pan. Cook till peas are tender.
3. Add coconut and a cup of water. Cook for another 5-10 minutes.
4. Add lime juice, salt and sugar. Bring to boil and remove it from the fire.
5. Serve hot with boiled rice.

Peas with Cottage Cheese
Khoa Matar

Serves : 4
Preparation Time : 20 mins.
Cooking Time : 20 mins.

Ingredients

Khoa 1 cup	Ghee 4 tbsp
Shelled peas 2 cups	Cumin seeds 1 tbsp
Tomatoes 2 medium	Turmeric powder ¼ tsp
Onions 2 small	Coriander seeds 1 tbsp
Green chillies 2-3	Garam masala ½ tsp
Red chilli powder ½ tsp	Salt to taste

Method

1. Wash all the vegetables.
2. Roast and grind cumin and coriander seeds.
3. Blanch the tomatoes and remove their skins.
4. Chop onions and green chillies.
5. Heat ghee in a pan, fry the onions and add the dry powders, and tomato pulp.
6. Cook for a minute, then add peas, one cup of water and salt.
7. Cook till peas are tender.
8. Then add khoa. Cook for 10 minutes or till water dries up.
9. Remove from the fire. Serve hot with puris or chapatis.

Lotus Stem Balls

Kamalkakri Koftas

Serves : 4
Preparation Time : 15 mins.
Cooking Time : 30 mins.

Ingredients

Kamalkakri 500 gm	Turmeric powder ¼ tsp
Onions 3	Tomatoes 2 large
Green chillies 2	Ghee for frying
Besan 2 tbsp	Red chilli powder to taste
Ginger, ground 1 cm piece	Salt to taste

Method

1. Peel kamalkakri and wash.
2. Boil in a pressure cooker in salted water for 3-4 minutes or till tender.
3. Drain the water and mash or grind into a smooth paste.
4. Mix it with besan, $^1/_2$ tsp of salt, ground green chillies and one finely chopped onion.
5. Make small balls of the mixture and deep fry them on slow heat till golden brown.
6. Remove them from the ghee and keep them aside.
7. Heat 2 tbsp ghee in a pan, add 2 ground onions and salt, fry till golden brown.

8. Add ginger, chilli powder, turmeric and chopped tomatoes.
9. Cook for 1-2 minutes. Add one glass of water and cook till the ghee separates or until gravy is thick.
10. Add fried koftas and cook on slow fire for 2-3 minutes.
11. Stir lightly to avoid the breakage of koftas.
12. Serve hot.

Brinjal Mash
Baingan ka Bhurta

Serves : 4
Preparation Time : 15 mins.
Cooking Time : 25 mins.

Ingredients

Brinjals 2 large, round

Onions 2 medium

Tomatoes 4 large

Ginger 2-cm piece

Red chilli powder 1 tsp

Ghee 2 tbsp

Salt to taste

Method

1. Roast the brinjals on burning coal or gas.
2. Peel and mash them.
3. Slice the onions and grind the ginger.
4. Heat ghee and fry onions and ginger.
5. Add brinjals and finely chopped tomatoes, chilli powder and salt.
6. Keep cooking and stirring until ghee separates and shows up.
7. Remove it from the fire.
8. Serve hot with chapatis.

SPICY FRIED POTATOES
DUM AALOO

Serves : 4
Preparation Time : 30 mins.
Cooking Time : 40 mins.

INGREDIENTS

Potatoes, medium sized 500 gm	Onions, ground 2 large
Red chilli powder 1 tsp	Ginger, ground 1-cm piece
Turmeric powder 1 tsp	Garlic, ground 1 pod
Curd 2 tbsp	Green chillies 2-3
Garam masala 1 tsp	Ghee 200 gm
Coriander seeds 2 tbsp	Coriander leaves 1 sprig
Cumin seeds 1 tsp	Salt to taste
Khus-khus 2 tbsp	

METHOD

1. Peel potatoes and prick them all over with a fork. Soak them in salted water for half an hour.
2. Roast khus-kh s and coriander and cumin seeds on a griddle and grind to a powder.
3. Heat the ghee in a pan and deep fry the potatoes till golden brown. Keep them aside.
4. In the same ghee, fry ground garlic, ginger and onions, green chillies and add roasted powders too.
5. Add turmeric, red chilli powder, salt and garam masala. Keep stirring till the masala begins to thicken.

6. Add one and a half cups of water, simmer till the masala is done and ghee shows up.
7. Then add potatoes and curd.
8. Cook for another 10-15 minutes on a very gentle heat.
9. Serve garnished with chopped coriander leaves.

Dry Potatoes
Aaloo Bhaji

Serves : 2
Preparation Time : 10 mins.
Cooking Time : 20 mins.

Ingredients

Potatoes, medium sized 250 gm	Cumin seeds 1 tsp
Onions 2 medium	Turmeric powder 1 tsp
Green chillies 3-4	Ghee 2 tbsp
Green coriander ½ bunch	Mango powder 1 tsp
Mustard powder ½ tsp	Salt to taste

Method

1. Boil, peel, and cut the potatoes into four pieces.
2. Slice the onions and chop the green chillies and coriander leaves. Heat ghee in a frying pan and add onions, cumin seeds, mustard powder, green chillies, turmeric and salt. Cook till onions become light brown.
3. Then add potatoes and sprinkle mango powder over it. Stir and leave it on the fire for 5 minutes.
4. Sprinkle chopped green coriander leaves and remove it from the fire. Serve with plain puris.

Mixed Vegetable Curry
Milijuli Sabzi

Serves : 4
Preparation Time : 15 mins.
Cooking Time : 20 mins.

Ingredients

Cauliflower 1 small	Carrots 2 large
Peas, shelled 100 gm	Onions 2 medium
Pumpkin 100 gm	Garlic ½ pod
Ginger 2-cm piece	Coriander powder 1 tsp
Ghee 2 tbsp	Turmeric powder 1 tsp
Green chillies 4-5	Tomato puree ½ cup
Potatoes 2 large	Salt to taste

Method

1. Wash, peel or scrape the vegetables.
2. Slice the onions. Cut the vegetables into pieces. Heat the ghee in a pan, add sliced onions and fry them till golden brown.
3. Add ground ginger and garlic, chopped green chillies, turmeric, coriander powder and salt. Fry for 2-3 minutes or till ghee separate from the masala. Then add all the vegetables and saute for 2-3 mins.
4. Add 2 cups of water and cook on a slow fire till tender. When tender, add tomato puree and allow it to cook till a thick gravy is formed.
5. Serve hot with plain parathas or chapatis.

POTATO AND CHEESE CURRY
AALOO-PANEER KI CURRY

Serves : 4
Preparation Time : 10 mins.
Cooking Time : 30 mins.

INGREDIENTS

Cottage cheese 200 gm	Cumin powder 1 tsp
Ghee for deep frying	Coriander powder 1 tsp
Potatoes 4-6 large	Red chilli powder 1 tsp or to taste
Tomatoes 3 medium	Water 3 cups
Onions 2 large	Coriander leaves 1 sprig
Turmeric powder 1 tsp	Salt to taste

METHOD

1. Cut cheese into small cubes and deep fry them in ghee till light brown. Keep them aside.
2. Brown onions in 3 tbsp of ghee.
3. Add chopped tomatoes, turmeric, salt, cumin powder, coriander powder and red chilli powder. Cook till tomatoes are soft and gravy is thick.
4. Add 3 to 3½ cups of water and let it boil.
5. Peel the potatoes and cut them into 4-6 pieces. Put potatoes into the pan and cook till tender.
6. Add fried cheese and cook for 5-6 mins. When gravy is thick, remove it from the fire. Serve garnished with chopped coriander leaves.

Peas and Mushroom Curry
Matar aur Mushroom ki Curry

Serves : 4
Preparation Time : 15 mins.
Cooking Time : 15 mins.

Ingredients

Fresh mushrooms 250 gm	Green chillies 2
Peas, shelled ½ kg	Green coriander 1 tbsp
Tomatoes 2	Sugar 1 tsp
Ginger 2-cm piece	Butter or ghee 3 tbsp
Water 1 cup	Coriander seeds 1 tsp
Salt, pepper & red chilli powder to taste	

Method

1. Wash, trim and cut mushrooms into quarters.
2. Grind ginger, green chillies and coriander seeds to a paste.
3. Blanch tomatoes and strain them to make a tomato pulp.
4. Heat butter in a pan, fry the masala paste till it turns brown, and add tomato pulp.
5. Add peas, mushrooms, red chilli powder, salt and sugar. Cook for 3-4 minutes.
6. Add one cup water. Cook it on a slow fire till peas are tender and gravy is thick. Sprinkle black pepper and coriander leaves. Serve hot.

Rice & Breads

Rice is a very special food for most Indian families. Easy to cook and easy to digest, rice can be prepared in a number of ways. It can be served as a pulao with curd or plain rice with a combination of vegetables. It not only makes a proper meal, but also makes a sweet dish for many occasions.

Some points to be taken into consideration while cooking rice:

1. *Clean the rice properly, wash it well and soak it in double its weight of water for cooking. Use the same water for cooking for full food value.*
2. *While making pulao, fry the rice in ghee for 2-3 minutes before adding the water.*

   Cook on medium heat till half of the water dries up. Then cover the pan and reduce the heat till the remaining water dries up. After that put a thick griddle under the pan and keep it on a slow fire for another ten minutes.

3. *Do not stir or use a spoon frequently.*

Wheat flour, gram flour, or rice flour are different kinds of flour most frequently used in an Indian kitchen in some form or the other. Chapatis, paranthas, puris, and dosas are prepared on different occasions. Wheat and gram flour are very rich in proteins, and rice flour is rich in carbohydrates.

Paranthas or puris can be eaten with a wide range of vegetables, dals, and curd.

Pea Pulao
Matar Pulao

Serves : 8
Preparation Time : 30 mins.
Cooking Time : 25 mins.

Ingredient

Rice 2 cups	Cloves 5-6
Ghee 4 tbsp	Garam masala 1 tsp
Shelled peas 1½ cups	Cardamoms 2
Onions 2 medium	Cumin seeds 1 tsp
Water 4 cups	Salt 1 tbsp
Cloves of garlic, chopped 10	

Method

1. Clean, wash and soak the rice for half an hour. Heat the ghee in a pan and fry the onions till brown.
2. Add peas, garlic, cardamoms, cumin seeds, cloves and garam masala. Cook for 5-6 minutes.
3. Add drained rice and salt and fry for 2-3 minutes.
4. Then add 4 cups of water and cook on a medium fire till half of the water dries up.
5. Reduce the heat to low and cook till the water dries up completely. Remove it from the fire but keep it covered for about 10 minutes.
6. Serve garnished with fried onions and sliced tomatoes. Curd can be served with it.

VEGETABLE PULAO WITH TOMATOES
TAMATAR PULAO

Serves : 8
Preparation Time : 30 mins.
Cooking Time : 25 mins.

INGREDIENTS

Rice 2 cups	Cardamoms 2
Shelled peas 50 gm	Cloves 3-4
Beans 100 gms	Cinnamon 1 -cm piece
Cauliflower 100 gm	Bayleaf 1
Tomatoes 4-5 medium	Pepper ½ tsp
Onion 1 medium	Salt to taste
Ghee 2-3 tbsp	

METHOD

1. Clean and soak rice for half an hour. Chop beans, cauliflower and tomatoes. Slice onion.
2. Heat ghee and fry onion till golden brown.
3. Add vegetables and fry for about 3-4 minutes.
4. Add cardamoms, cloves, cinnamon, bayleaf, pepper and salt.
5. Cook for two minutes and add rice and 4 cups of water.
6. Bring to boil and then cook on a low fire.
7. Cover with the lid till rice is cooked. Serve hot with curd.

TAMARIND RICE
KHATTE CHAWAL

Serves : 8
Preparation Time : 15 mins.
Cooking Time : 10 mins.

INGREDIENTS

Rice 2 cups	Red chilli powder 1 tsp
Tamarind pulp 2 tbsp	Onions 2 medium
Mustard seeds 1 tbsp	Oil or ghee 4 tbsp
Turmeric powder 1 tbsp	Salt to taste

METHOD

1. Boil rice in twice the amount of water for one minute, in a pressure cooker.
2. Heat oil in a frying pan. Fry onions till golden brown, add mustard seeds, then tamarind pulp, turmeric, red chilli powder and salt.
3. Cook till oil separates.
4. Spread rice in a flat dish. Pour the above mixture over the rice.
5. Mix with a fork and serve.

Mushroom and Capsicum Pulao
Simla Mirch aur Guchchi Pulao

Serves	:	8
Preparation Time	:	15 mins.
Cooking Time	:	25 mins.

Ingredients

- Rice 2 cups
- Mushrooms 200 gm
- Capsicums 6 medium
- Onions 2 large
- Ghee 4 tbsp
- Bay leaves 2
- Lime juice 2 tsp
- Salt & pepper to taste

Method

1. Wash and cut mushrooms into quarters. Cut capsicums into rounds, removing pith and seeds.
2. Clean, wash and drain the rice.
3. Heat ghee, fry onions till golden brown. Add mushroom and capsicum and saute them for 3-4 minutes on low heat.
4. Add bay leaves, salt, pepper and rice. Fry for another two minutes and add 4 cups of water. Stir once gently and cover. Cook till rice is tender. Then place a thick griddle underneath the pan.
5. Finally sprinkle lime juice and remove the pan from the fire. Serve hot with curd.

Pongal Rice
Pongal Chawal

Serves	:	8
Preparation Time	:	10 mins.
Cooking Time	:	20 mins.

Ingredients

Rice 2 cups

Cashewnuts 1 tbsp

Coconut, grated ½

Raisins 1 tbsp

Cardamom powder 2 tbsp

Ghee 8 tbsp

Salt to taste

Method

1. Clean, wash and drain the rice. Fry the cashewnuts and raisins in 2 tbsp of ghee.
2. Pour in 4 cups of water and add salt too. When the water starts boiling add the rice and cover the pan.
3. When the rice is half cooked, add the grated coconut, cardamom powder and the rest of the ghee.
4. Cover the pan again and cook the rice on slow fire till tender.
5. Serve cold or hot.

Luchis

Makes : 10
Preparation Time : 45 mins.
Cooking Time : 15 mins.

Ingredients

- Wheat flour 2 cups
- Water ½ cup
- Ghee 2 tbsp & for frying
- Salt to taste

Method

1. Mix flour, ghee, water and salt and make a stiff dough. Knead it well. Keep it aside for at least half an hour.
2. Knead it again till it is soft enough to roll.
3. Make small balls and roll out into rounds.
4. Heat the ghee in a frying pan when it is hot, deep fry the rolled rounds of flour.
5. Take them out when golden brown.
6. Place them directly on a brown sheet of paper.
7. Serve hot with chana or any other vegetable.

Bhaturas

Makes : 15

Preparation Time : 4½ mins.
Cooking Time : 40 mins.

INGREDIENTS

Maida 2 cups	Sugar 1 tsp
Curd 120 gm	Ghee for frying
Soda bi-carbonate 1 tbsp	Salt to taste
Warm water 7-8 tbsp	

METHOD

1. Mix the flour, soda bi-carbonate and salt. Since them together.
2. Add sugar, curd and warm water and make a stiff dough. Continue kneading the dough till it stops sticking to the fingers.
3. Cover it with a wet cloth and leave if for 4 hours atleast.
4. Divide th dough into 15 equal parts. Shape them into balls.
5. Flatten the balls with the palm of the hand and roll out into a shape of chapati.
6. Fry them one at a time in smoking hot ghee till light brown. Bhatures are generally served with khatta kabuli chanas.

Paranthas Stuffed with Cauliflower

Gobhiwala Paranthas

Makes	:	10
Preparation Time	:	45 mins.
Cooking Time	:	45 mins.

INGREDIENTS

- Flour 1½ cups
- Cauliflower 1 small
- Water ¼ cup
- Ghee 2-3 tbsp and for frying
- Salt and red chillis to taste

METHOD

1. Wash and remove the stem and grate the cauliflower.
2. Heat 2 tbsp of ghee in a pan, add grated cauliflower, salt and red chillis.
3. Saute for 2-3 minutes and remove it from the fire.
4. Prepare the dough as for plain paranthas. Divide into small balls. Roll them into small balls.
5. Place some stuffing in the center and enclose it well.
6. Roll out gentally.
7. Heat a griddle and shallow fry them on the hot griddle by adding little ghee at a time around the edges till paranthas get golden brown.
8. Serve hot with curd.

Puris

Makes : 15
Preparation Time : 1½ hr.
Cooking Time : 30 mins.

Ingredients

Wheat flour 1 cup

Flour 1 cup

Ghee 2 tsp & tor deep frying

Salt ½ tsp

Method

1. Sieve flours and salt together in a flat dish.
2. Add ghee and mix it well with the fingers.
3. Add water and make a stiff dough.
4. Knead thoroughly till the dough is smooth and soft. Cover it with a damp muslin cloth and leave for an hour or so. Knead it again.
5. Divide the dough into small balls.
6. Roll them out thinly into small rounds.
7. Heat the ghee in a frying pan. Deep fry them in hot ghee.
8. When frying, press them on top so they swell up.
9. Remove when light brown on both sides. Serve hot.

PURE STUFFED WITH URAD DAL
URAD DAL KI PURI

Makes	:	12
Preparation Time	:	Overnight
Cooking Time	:	40 mins.

INGREDIENTS

Wheat flour 1½ cups	Water ½ cup
Urad dal ½ cup	Ghee 2 tbsp & for deep frying
Red chillis ½ tsp	Salt to taste
Cumin seeds ½ tsp	

METHOD

1. Soak the dal in water overnight. Drain and grind to a fine paste. Heat 2 tbsp of ghee and fry dal paste till dry.
2. Then mix in cumin seeds, chillis and salt.
3. Combine wheat flour, 2 tbsp of ghee, salt and water to make a dough.
4. Knead it well and make a stiff dough. Cover it with a damp cloth and keep it aside for half an hour.
5. Then make small-sized balls and flatten them a bit with the palm of your hand. Put 1 tbsp dal mixture in the flattened ball.
6. Pinch the edges together to form a ball again. Roll out into 5 cm rounds.
7. Heat the ghee and deep fry these puris till light brown and puffed. Take them out directly on a brown sheet of paper. Serve them hot.

Plain Dosa
Sada Dosa

Makes	:	15
Preparation Time	:	32 hrs
Cooking Time	:	15 mins.

Ingredients

Rice 1 cup	Ghee for shallow frying
Black gram dal split ½ cup	Salt 1 tsp
Fenugreek seeds ½ tsp	

Method

1. Clean rice and dal. Soak rice and dal for about 20 hours.
2. Drain water. Grind rice and dal together to a smooth paste.
3. Add a little water and make a batter of pouring consistency.
4. Mix salt and fenugreek seeds in it and leave this batter for about 12 hours.
5. Heat a thick griddle and spread a little ghee over it.
6. Drop a big spoonful of batter in the centre and quickly start spreading it.
7. Cook it on a low fire for about half a minute.
8. Turn it over and fry the other side till light brown and crisp. Serve hot with sambar.

Dosa Stuffed with Potatoes
Masala Dosa

Makes	:	15
Preparation Time	:	Overnight
Cooking Time	:	25 mins.

Ingredients

For the Batter

Rice 1 cup	Black gram dal split ½ cup
Fenugreek seeds 1 tsp	Salt to taste

For the Filling

Boiled potatoes 5-6 medium	Turmeric powder ½ tsp
Boiled peas 4 tbsp	Green chillies 2
Onion 1 small	Salt to taste

Method

1. Clean rice and dal. Soak for about 12 hours.
2. Drain water and grind into a smooth paste.
3. Add a little water and make the batter of pouring consistency.
4. Mix in salt and fenugreek seeds.
5. Chop onion, fry in ghee, add salt, green chillies and turmeric.
6. Add boiled, chopped potatoes and boiled peas. Cook for 2-3 minutes and remove from the fire.

7. Then heat a thick griddle.
8. Put a big spoonful of batter on it.
9. Spread it fast and put a tbsp ghee around the dosa.
10. Place the cooked vegetable (2 tbsp) in the centre.
11. Cook for 2-3 minutes, then turn both the sides to the centre and cook the other side.
12. Remove it from the griddle with a flat spoon.
13. Serve hot with coconut chutney.

Curd Recipes

Different combinations and flavours can be added to the curd to make delicious raitas. It adds colour to a dish. It simulates the appetite, promotes digestion, and is very filling too.

MARROW RAITA
GHIA KA RAITA

Serves	:	4
Preparation Time	:	15 mins.
Cooking Time	:	10 mins.

INGREDIENTS

- Curd 2 cups
- Marrow 150 gms
- Ground mustard seeds ½ tsp
- Roasted, ground cumin seeds ½ tsp
- Pepper and salt to taste

METHOD

1. Peel and grate the marrow.
2. Boil the grated marrow in sufficient water. Cook it till tender.
3. Strain the boiled marrow.
4. Beat the curd well in a bowl, add ground mustard seeds, pepper, salt and mix well.
5. Add marrow and mix.
6. Garnish it with ground cumin seeds and serve.

Potato and Tomato Raita
Aaloo Tamatar ka Raita

Serves	:	4
Preparation Time	:	15 mins.
Cooking Time	:	10 mins.

Ingredients

- Curd 2 cups
- Potatoes 2 medium
- Tomatoes 2 small
- Roasted, ground cumin seeds ½ tsp
- Coriander leaves ¼ bunch
- Salt & pepper to taste

Method

1. Boil, peel and chop the potatoes.
2. Chop tomatoes also.
3. Beat curd and mix salt, pepper and cumin seed powder.
4. Add chopped potatoes and tomatoes and mix it well.
5. Pour the raita in a bowl and garnish it with coriander leaves and ground cumin seeds.
6. Serve with plain paranthas.

Boondi ka Raita

Serves	:	4
Preparation Time	:	10 mins.
Cooking Time	:	10 mins.

Ingredients

Curd 2 cups
Bengal gram flour (besan) 4 tbsp
Water 5-6 tbsp
Ghee for frying
Salt and pepper to taste

Method

1. Mix besan with water to make a batter of dropping consistency.
2. Beat the batter well and mix in a pinch of salt.
3. Heat ghee in a frying pan to smoking point.
4. With frying spoon drop batter into pan through holes.
5. Fry till golden brown.
6. Remove boondi from the ghee and dip it into water for about 10 minutes.
7. Remove from the water and squeeze gently.
8. Add spices to beaten curd.
9. Add boondi, mix it well and sprinkle pepper and serve.

Dahi Baras

Serves	:	4
Preparation Time	:	Overnight
Cooking Time	:	20 mins.

Ingredients

Curd 3 cups

Urad dal 1 cup

Green chillies 2-3

Onion 1 large

Red chilli powder ½ tsp

Salt and garam masala to taste

Method

1. Soak dal overnight.
2. Drain and grind it into a fine paste.
3. Beat it, adding 1-2 tbsp of curd or water.
4. Continue beating it until foamy and light. To test whether it is light, drop a little into a bowl of water. If it rises to the top, it is light enough.
5. Then add chopped onion, green chillies, garam masala, red chilli powder, and salt.
6. Mix well and allow it to stand for half an hour.
7. Spread a piece of wet muslin cloth over a bowl.
8. Take 1 tbsp of the mixture and put it on the cloth and make baras.

9. Heat ghee in a frying pan and fry baras on a low fire till they are golden brown. Then put them into hot water.
10. Squeeze out the extra water and keep them ready.
11. Beat curd till smooth and mix in salt and pepper.
12. Dip baras in it and arrange them in a flat dish.

Spinach Raita
Palak ka Raita

Serves : 8
Preparation Time : 20 mins.
Cooking Time : 10 mins.

Ingredients

- Curd 6 cups
- Spinach 500 gms
- Cumin seeds ½ tbsp
- Salt & pepper to taste

Method

1. Wash the spinach well and boil it for about 10 minutes.
2. Then drain it and grind it into a fine paste.
3. Beat curd well, add salt and pepper.
4. Mix the ground spinach in it.
5. Roast the cumin seeds and grind them well.
6. Sprinkle cumin powder over the raita before serving.

Desserts and Indian Sweets

No meal is complete without a dessert. Our sweet dishes are unique. The use of cardamoms, saffron and nuts make sweet dishes extremely delicious and give them an exquisite appearance. Indian sweet dishes are generally associated with religious ceremonies, as atta or suji halwa is served by Sikhs on ceremonial occasions, kheer is made by Hindus for their religious gatherings and sewian are prepared by the Muslims on their festivals.

Halwa can also be prepared from vegetables. It should always be served hot. Here a few baked desserts are also included and they can be enjoyed by both children and grown-ups.

Indian sweets can be served as desserts as well as snacks, and can be prepared from flour, milk and curd. Since quite a number of them can be well preserved, they can be stored and offered to unexpected guests. These recipes are very easy and quick to prepare.

ZARDA

ZARDA CHAWAL

Serves : 6
Preparation Time : 15 mins.
Cooking Time : 30 mins.

INGREDIENTS

Rice 1 cup	Ghee 4 tbsp
Chopped almonds 4 tbsp	Cardamoms 4-5
Sugar ¾ cup	Cloves 4
Yellow colour a few drops	Raisins 4 tbsp
Silver papers 2	

METHOD

1. Wash and soak the rice for 10 minutes in 2 cups of water.
2. Heat the ghee, add cloves, cardamom seeds and skins and fry for 1-2 minutes. Add rice and water in which rice was soaked. Cook till the rice becomes soft.
3. Add sugar and yellow colour and cook till sugar is fully dissolved and well mixed. Add a few chopped almonds and soaked and drained raisins.
4. Cover and put the pan on a thick griddle for another 10 minutes. Remove from the fire. Decorate with silver papers and the rest of the chopped almonds.
5. Serve hot.

RICE - PAYASAM
PAYASAM CHAWAL

Serves : 6
Preparation Time : 10 mins
Cooking Time : 30 mins

INGREDIENTS

Rice 8 tbsp

Milk 1 ltr

Almonds, chopped 1 tbsp

Raisins 1 tbsp

Cardamom powder 1 tsp

Jaggery 8 tbsp

METHOD

1. Wash and drain the rice.
2. Boil the milk in a pan.
3. Add the rice - preferbly broken . Keep cooking on a medium fire.
4. When the rice is half cooked , add the almonds , raisins and jaggery.
5. Continue cooking on a low fire till the rice is fully cooked.
6. Add cardamom powder last and remove it from the fire.
7. Serve hot

PHIRNI

Serves : 6
Preparation Time : 40 mins
Cooking Time : 30 mins

INGREDIENTS

Milk 1 ltr

Rice ½ cup

Sugar 3/4 cup

Powdered cardamom 1 tsp

Pistachio nuts 2-3 tbsp

Silver paper 2

METHOD

1. Wash and soak the rice for half an hour.
2. Boil milk with pistachio nuts.
3. Drain water from rice and grind the rice either very fine or thick as desired.
4. Make a paste of the rice adding 2-3 tbsp of water.
5. When milk boils , add this paste to it and keep stirring.
6. Continue cooking till the mixture thickness.
7. Add sugar and cook for 5-7 minutes more.
8. Add powdered cardamom and remove it from the fire Serve hot or cold. Garnish with silver papers.

SWEET POTATO KHEER
SHAKARKANDI KI KHEER

Serves : 6
Preparation Time : 15 mins.
Cooking Time : 25 mins.

INGREDIENTS

Milk 7-8 cups

Sweet potatoes 250 gm

Sugar 1 cup

Almonds blanched and chopped 4 tbsp

METHOD

1. Skin the sweet potatoes and grate them or cut them into very fine pieces.
2. Put milk in a pan, add sweet potatoes and cook on a low fire, stirring occasionally.
3. When milk starts getting thick, add sugar and chopped almonds.
4. Simmer for another 5-10 minutes until the mixture becomes thick like custard.
5. Remove it from the fire.
6. This kheer can be served cold as well as hot.

Atta Halwa

Serves : 6
Preparation Time : 5 mins.
Cooking Time : 20 mins.

Ingredients

Atta (or whole wheat (lour) 1 cup

Sugar ¾ cup

Ghee ¾ cup

Almonds, blanched and chopped 1 tbsp

Raisins 1 tbsp

Water 2½ cups

Method

1. Make syrup with sugar and water.
2. Bring it to a boil till it makes one thread syrup. Keep it aside.
3. Sift flour well.
4. In a frying pan heat ghee, add flour and fry till it becomes light brown.
5. Pour the sugar-syrup into it and keep stirring it continuously.
6. Cook till the mixture starts leaving the side of the pan.
7. Remove it from the fire, garnish with chopped nuts and serve hot.

Carrot Halwa

Gajar ka Halwa

Serves	:	12
Preparation Time	:	30 mins.
Cooking Time	:	40 mins.

Ingredients

Carrots 1 kg	Shredded almonds 12
Milk 6 cups	Ghee 3 tbsp
Khoya 150 gm	Silver papers 2
Sugar 175 gm	

Method

1. Wash, scrape and grate the carrots.
2. Heat ghee in a frying pan add carrots and fry for 5 minutes. Cover and cook on a low fire for 5-10 minutes.
3. Add khoya and milk to the carrots.
4. Cook it on a low fire, stirring occasionally, till the milk is completely absorbed.
5. Add sugar and cook till it dissolves.
6. Cook for about 3-4 minutes till the halwa is nearly dry.
7. Mix well and take the pan off the fire.
8. Garnish with silver papers and shredded almonds.

Moong Dal Halwa
Moong ki Dal ka Halwa

Serves	:	4
Preparation Time	:	10 hrs.
Cooking Time	:	30 mins.

Ingredients

Green gram dal 150 gm	Ghee 8 tbsp
Sugar 200 gm	Chopped almonds 3 tbsp
Milk 2 cups	Cardamom powder ½, tsp
Khoya 200 gm	Chopped raisins 2 tbsp

Method

1. Clean and soak dal in water for 8-10 hours. Drain and grind to a paste.
2. Add sugar to milk and boil it on the fire till the sugar is dissolved.
3. Put ghee in a pan and fry the dal paste on a low fire till the colour becomes golden.
4. Add milk and cook for a few minutes more.
5. Then add khoya and cook on a low fire, stirring continuously, till the khoya is completely absorbed in the mixture.
6. Then add the almonds, raisins and cardamom powder.
7. Serve hot.

Gulab Jamun

Serves : 8
Preparation Time : 20 mins.
Cooking Time : 20 mins.

Ingredients

- Khoya 300 gm
- Flour (maida) 100 gm
- Sugar 250 gm
- Water 100 gm

Method

1. Make the syrup with sugar and water. It should be of one thread consistency.
2. Rub the khoya to softness to free the granules.
3. Then add flour and mix it well to make a soft dough.
4. Make 1-cm diameter balls.
5. Deep fry them on a low fire. Fry till deep brown.
6. Then remove the balls from the ghee and immediately dip them in the sugar syrup.
7. Let the balls soak for half an hour. Then serve hot or cold.

COCONUT MYSORE PAK
NARIAL MYSORE PAK

Serves : 6
Preparation Time : 5 mins.
Cooking Time : 20 mins.

INGREDIENTS

- Sugar 1 cup
- Ghee 2½ cups
- Coconut powder 1 cup
- Water ½ cup

METHOD

1. Mix sugar and water and bring it to a boil till it makes one thread syrup.
2. Then add coconut powder and ghee to it.
3. Continue cooking, and stirring constantly till the mixture changes colour to a very light brown and starts leaving the sides of the pan.
4. Turn into a greased tray.
5. Cool it for a few minutes and cut into square pieces.

Banana-Apple Betty

Serves : 6
Preparation Time : 15 mins.
Cooking Time : 45 mins.

Ingredients

Sugar ¾ cup

Apples 2

Bananas 3-4

Bread cubes 3 cups

Butter 3 tbsp

Cinnamon powder ½ tsp

Salt ½ tsp

Method

1. Mix sugar, salt and cinnamon powder together.
2. Combine with sliced apples and bananas.
3. Fry bread cubes in butter till they are golden brown.
4. Fill greased baking dish with alternate layers of bread cubes and fruit.
5. Make the topmost and bottom layers with the bread cubes.
6. Cover the dish and bake in a moderate oven for ½ an hour.
7. Then uncover the dish and bake for another 10 minutes.

Peach Betty

Serves : 6.
Preparation Time : 20 mins.
Cooking Time : 45 mins.

Ingredients

Bread crumbs 2 cups

Melted butter 2 tbsp

Sliced fresh peaches 2 cups

Water 4 tbsp

Lemon juice 2 tbsp

Lemon rind ½ tsp

Sugar ½ cup

Method

1. Moisten crumbs with butter.
2. Place alternate layers of crumbs and peaches in a greased baking dish.
3. Make the first layer with crumbs and then the last again with crumbs.
4. Mix lemon juice, lemon rind and water.
5. Sprinkle each layer of peaches with the lemon mixture and 2 tbsp of sugar.
6. Bake for about 40-45 minutes on a low heat.

CHHENNA MURKI

Serves : 4-5
Preparation Time : 10 mins.
Cooking Time : 20 mins.

INGREDIENTS

- Cheese 250 gm
- Sugar 115 gm
- Water 100 ml
- Kewra essence 2 to 3 drops
- Silver papers 2-3

METHOD

1. Shape the cheese into square pieces.
2. Mix the sugar and water and cook over a low fire till it is of one thread consistency.
3. Add the cheese cubes to the syrup and cook until they are coated with syrup.
4. Remove from the fire, add essence and roll the pan until the cubes are thickly coated with sugar and separate from each other.
5. Put them in a plate, decorate with silver paper, and serve.

Coconut Burfi
Narial ki Burfi

Serves : 4-6
Preparation Time : 5 mins.
Cooking Time : 25 mins.

INGREDIENTS

Coconut powder 1 cup	Suga 1 cup
Milk 4 cups	Pink colour a few drops
Butter 1 tbsp	Any essence a few drops

Method

1. Melt butter in a pan and add milk and sugar.
2. Stir until the sugar dissolves.
3. Simmer for 10 minutes, then add the coconut powder.
4. Do not cease stirring until the mixture has formed into a thick paste.
5. Spread half a tsp. of the mixture on a plate.
6. Cool and roll it with a finger. If it rolls well, leaving the plate clean, then the burfi is ready to be taken off the stove. Just before taking the burfi off, add the essence and pink colour.
7. Mix it thoroughly and pour into a greased flat dish.
8. Cool and cut into square pieces.

Sweet Rice Burfi
Chawal ki Burfi

Serves	:	4-6
Preparation Time	:	5 mins.
Cooking Time	:	40 mins.

Ingredients

Rice 1 cup	Ghee ½ cup
Sugar 2 cups	Cardamom powder 1 tsp
Water 1 cup	Chopped almonds 1 tbsp
Saffron powder 1/4 tsp	Raisins 100 gm

Method

1. Wash and boil the rice till half-cooked.
2. Cook the sugar in water, stirring continuously, till it becomes one thread consistency.
3. Add rice, raisins, almonds and ghee.
4. Stir with the back of the spoon and see that it does not stick to the bottom.
5. Add saffron and cardamom powder, stir again and see if rice is cooked.
6. Remove from the fire. Spread on greased plates.
7. When cool, cut to any shape.

Besan Laddoos
Besan ke Laddoo

Serves : 8-10
Preparation Time : 5 mins.
Cooking Time : 40 mins.

Ingredients

Gram flour (besan) 2 cups	Ghee 2 cups
Flour ½ cup	Cashewnuts chopped 200 gm
Sugar 2½ cups	Cardamom powder 1 tsp
Water 2 cups	

Method

1. Make a thin syrup with the sugar and water.
2. Put the ghee in a frying pan.
3. When it is burning hot, add besan to it.
4. Fry till it starts smelling and changes its colour.
5. Add the sugar syrup to it.
6. Add the cardamom powder and cashewnuts.
7. Cook it, stirring constantly, till it becomes thick and the ghee leaves the sides of the pan. Remove it from the fire.
8. Shape in the form of laddoos and serve.

Snacks & Soft Drinks

There is nothing like home made snacks served fresh with morning coffee, evening tea or cocktails. Of course there are snacks to make and keep for eating in between meals or while travelling. Snacks bought from the market may be full of preservatives besides being very expensive. Recipes given here take only a few minutes to prepare. They are delicious when served with chutney or sauces.

Squashes and sharbats should be made only when the fruit or vegetable is in plenty and in season.

Special care should be taken while preserving the squashes and sharbats. Bottles should be properly cleaned, sterilised and dry.

FRIED PULSES
BHUNNI DAL

Serves	:	4-6
Preparation Time	:	5 hrs.
Cooking Time	:	15 mins.

INGREDIENTS

- Chana or Moong dal 250 gm
- Ghee for frying
- Salt to taste

METHOD

1. Soak the dal for 4-5 hours and then drain it.
2. Spread dal on a paper. Heat the ghee in a pan and place a little dal in a sieve.
3. Dip the sieve into hot ghee and deep fry.
4. When the bubbles stop, remove the sieve from the ghee and spread the fried dal directly on a sheet of brown paper or newspaper.
5. Rub the salt into the dal.
6. Cool it and preserve in a tin or plastic box to avoid moisture.

RICE CRISPIES
PHULWADI

Serves : 8-10
Preparation Time : 15 mins.
Cooking Time : 30 mins.

INGREDIENTS

Rice flour 250 gm

Suji 1 tbsp

Water 7-8 times of the rice quantity

Cumin seeds 1 tbsp

Ghee for frying

Salt to taste

METHOD

1. Boil water in a big pan, add rice flour, suji, salt and cumin seeds.
2. Cook till the flour is cooked.
3. Spread a white sheet in the sun.
4. Take the cooked mixture and pour tablespoons 4-cms apart on the sheet.
5. Leave them in the sun to dry.
6. When dry, wet the cloth on the reverse and remove the rice crispies by scraping them with a knife.
7. Deep fry them in hot ghee.
8. Serve them hot.

Semolina and Potato Wadas
Suji Aur Aaloo Wada

Serves : 10-12
Preparation Time : 3 hrs.
Cooking Time : 40 mins.

Ingredients

- Suji 200 gm
- Potatoes 1 kg
- Sagoo-dana 250 gm
- Green chillies 6-8
- Ghee for frying
- Salt to taste

Method

1. Soak sagoo-dana in water for about 2 hours and then drain it properly.
2. Mix mashed potatoes, sagoo-dana, suji, green chillies and salt together.
3. Leave for ½ hour.
4. Make small wadas with the mixture.
5. Deep fry them in the ghee on slow fire.
6. Take them out of the ghee directly on a sheet of brown paper or newspaper. The paper soaks up excess grease.
7. Serve them hot with mint chutney.

Mathi

Serves : 4-6
Preparation Time : 30 mins.
Cooking Time : 30 mins.

Ingredients

- Flour 250 gm
- Ghee 100 gm
- Ajwain 1 tsp
- Soda-bi-carb ½ tbsp
- Water ½ cup
- Salt ½ tbsp

Method

1. Mix all the ingredients with the fingers.
2. Make a stiff dough and knead for 5-7 minutes.
3. Cover with a wet cloth and leave aside.
4. Heat a little ghee in a frying pan.
5. Roll a portion of the dough in a circle.
6. Deep fry on a low fire and put them on brown paper to soak excess grease.
7. Make the rest of the mathis in the same manner.
8. When cool, store them in a box in a dry place.

Besan-Sev

Serves	:	4-6
Preparation Time	:	20 mins.
Cooking Time	:	30 mins.

Ingredients

- Besan 250 gm
- Soda-bi-carb 1 tbsp
- Red chilli powder 1 tbsp
- Water ½ cup
- Ghee for frying
- Salt 1 tbsp

Method

1. Sieve besan, soda-bicarb, salt and chilli powder together.
2. Mix all the ingredients and make a soft dough with sufficient water.
3. Heat ghee or oil in a frying pan.
4. Place a little of the dough in a potato-masher.
5. Press the masher in hot ghee or oil.
6. Fry till the bubbles stop, remove from the ghee.
7. When cool, store them in a box in a dry place.

Muthia

Serves : 8-10
Preparation Time : 1 hr.
Cooking Time : 30 mins.

Ingredients

Peas, unshelled 750 gm	Mango powder ½ tsp
Cabbage 100 gm	Oil ½ cup
Coriander leaves chopped 1 bunch	Atta or wheat flour 1 cup
Red chillis powder ¼ tsp	Besan or Bengal gram flour ½ cup
Turmeric powder ½ tsp	Suji 1/4 cup
Garam masala ¼ tsp	

Method

1. Chop cabbage finely, shell peas and grind them together to make a fine paste.
2. Mix all the flours and add oil to it. Rub the mixture well and add red chilli, turmeric, mango powders, garam masala and mix well.
3. Add cabbage-pea paste and chopped coriander leaves and mix it well.
4. Take a small quantity in hand and press to see whether it forms a ball. If not, then sprinkle a little water and make small balls with the mixture and put them in a big sieve.
5. Boil water in a big pan, place sieve on top and cover the pan to let it steam for half an hour. Muthias can be eaten just steamed or can be fried just before serving.

Besan ki Kakri

Serves	:	4-6
Preparation Time	:	10 mins.
Cooking Time	:	15 mins.

Ingredients

Besan 1 cup	Mango powder ¼ tsp
Ghee 2 tbsp	Garam masala ¼ tsp
Mustard seeds ¼ tsp	Red chilli powder ¼ tsp
Turmeric powder ¼ tsp	Asafoetida ⅛ tsp
Coriander powder ¼ tsp	Salt to taste
Tomatoes 2 medium	

Method

1. Heat ghee, put in asafoetida and add all the masalas.
2. Fry for a minute and then put in gram flour.
3. Stir-fry till it smells and turns light brown.
4. Add 2½ cups of water to make a thick paste.
5. Add chopped tomatoes. Cook till dry.
6. Grease a tray and spread this mixture on it.
7. Leave to set. Then cut into squares, and store them.

Samosas

Makes : 40
Preparation Time : 1 hr.
Cooking Time : 40 mins.

Ingredients

Maida 250 gm	Peas 100 gm
Ghee 60 gm	Green chillies chopped 2
Baking powder ½ tsp	Mango powder (amchur) 1 tbsp
Water 5-6 tbsp	Pepper 1 tsp
Salt ½ tsp	Ghee for frying
Potatoes 250 gm	Garam masala 1 tbsp
Onion chopped 1 medium	Salt 1 tsp

Method

1. Sieve together maida, baking powder and salt.
2. Rub the ghee into maida and make a stiff dough with maida and water.
3. For stuffing, peel potatoes and shell peas. Boil them. Heat the ghee and fry the onion, add green chillies, peas, potatoes, salt, pepper and mango powder.
4. Cook for 2-3 minutes, add garam masala and remove it from the fire.
5. Divide the dough into 20 equal parts. Shape them into balls.
6. Flatten the balls and roll them out into rounds. Then cut each round into two halves.

7. Moisten the edges of semi-circles, and make a funnel shape and fill it with the vegetable stuffing. Seal the edges with the moistened maida.
8. Deep fry them in hot ghee till crisp and golden brown on both sides.
9. Serve with tomato sauce or mint chutney.

Banana Fritters
Kele ki Tukri

Serves : 4-6
Preparation Time : 15 mins.
Cooking Time : 15 mins.

Ingredients

- Flour (maida) 1 cup
- Sugar 4 tbsp
- Baking powder 1 tbsp
- Ripe bananas 3-4
- Milk 1 cup
- Ghee for frying
- Butter 1 tbsp

Method

1. Sift flour and baking powder together.
2. Combine sugar, flour and milk together.
3. Beat it nicely till it makes a smooth batter.
4. Skin and chop bananas.
5. Add chopped bananas to the paste.
6. Drop a tablespoon of mixture into deep hot fat and fry till fritters become golden brown.
7. Serve them hot.

Cauliflower Pakoras
Gobhi ke Pakore

Serves : 3-4
Preparation Time : 15 mins.
Cooking Time : 20 mins.

Ingredients

Besan ½ cup	Water ¼ cup
Mango powder 1 tsp	Ghee for frying
Red chilli powder ½ tsp	Salt and pepper to taste
Cauliflower 1 medium	

Method

1. Make a smooth batter with besan and water.
2. Mix in salt, pepper, mango powder and red chilli powder.
3. Boil about two cups of water with ½ teaspoon of salt.
4. Cut the cauliflower into small pieces.
5. Put these pieces in water for about 2-3 mins.
6. Remove from the water and drain.
7. Beat the batter hard for five minutes to make it fluffy and creamy.
8. Dip each piece of the cauliflower and deep fry for a few minutes at a time. Serve hot with mint chutney.

CHIRWA

Serves : 4-6
Preparation Time : 5 mins.
Cooking Time : 10 mins.

INGREDIENTS

- Chirwa 1 cup
- Ghee 2-3 tbsp
- Green chillies 2 large
- Turmeric powder 1 pinch
- Peas, boiled 4 tbsp
- Mustard seeds 1 tsp
- Salt to taste

METHOD

1. Heat ghee in a pan.
2. Fry mustard seeds.
3. Add turmeric and chopped green chillies.
4. Fry for a minute, then add boiled peas, salt and washed chirwa.
5. Cook for 5 minutes stirring, continuously.
6. When done remove it from the fire.
7. Serve hot.

Sprouted Green Gram

Serves : 4-6
Preparation Time : 2 days
Cooking Time : 10 mins.

Ingredients

- Green gram whole 1 cup
- Onion 1 medium
- Green chillies chopped 3
- Ghee 2 tbsp
- Lime juice ½ tbsp
- Cumin seeds ½ tsp
- Salt and pepper to taste

Method

1. Clean and soak the green gram for about 24 hours.
2. Drain and hang in a muslin bag tied tightly for about another 24 hours or till the gram sprouts.
3. Heat ghee in a pan, chop onion and fry with cumin seeds till light brown. Add green chillies, salt and pepper too.
4. Cook for a minute and then add sprouted gram.
5. Stir fry for 5-7 minutes on a low fire.
6. Remove from the fire and add lime juice. Mix it well.
7. Serve hot or cold.

POTATO CUTLETS
AALOO KI TIKKI

Serves : 3-4
Preparation Time : 15 mins.
Cooking Time : 20 mins.

INGREDIENTS

Potatoes 250 gm	Bread crumbs 2 tbsp
Onions 2 small	Ghee for frying
Green chillies 3-4	Salt to tasle
Gram flour or besan 3-4 tbsp	

METHOD

1. Boil and peel potatoes.
2. Mash them well.
3. Mix in chopped onions, chopped green chillies and salt.
4. Take a little portion of the mixture and make small cutlets.
5. Make batter with besan, salt and water.
6. Keep beating till batter becomes smooth and creamy.
7. Dip the potato cutlets in the batter then, roll them in bread crumbs
8. Heat ghee and deep fry them on a low fire.
9. Serve hot with tomato sauce.

POTATO PATTIES

Serves	:	4-6
Preparation Time	:	15 mins.
Cooking Time	:	20 mins.

INGREDIENTS

Potatoes 500 gm	Garam masala ½ tsp
Slices of bread 10	Mango powder 1 tsp
Peas ¼ cup	Ghee for frying
Coriander powder ½ tsp	Salt to taste
Green chillies 3-4	

METHOD

1. Peel and boil potatoes and shell peas. Mix mashed potatoes, peas, coriander powder, diced green chillies, garam masala, salt and mango powder together.
2. Soak the bread slices in water. Press them lightly against the palm of your hand to squeeze out the extra water.
3. Take 2-3 tbsp of potato mixture. Put it in the centre of the slice as a filling. Close up and give it the shape of a patty.
4. Heat ghee and deep fry them till golden brown. Serve them hot with sauce.

VEGETABLE HOT-DOGS

Makes : 10
Preparation Time : 15 mins.
Cooking Time : 20 mins.

INGREDIENTS

Rolls 10	Onion sliced 1
Potatoes 250 gm	Tomato sliced 1
Green chillies chopped 3-4	Ghee for frying
Onions chopped 2 small	Salt to taste
Ginger chopped 1 tsp	

METHOD

1. Boil and mash the potatoes and chop the onions and green chillies.
2. Add onions, green chillies, ginger and potatoes and salt in a pan. Mix them well and make roll about 5-cm long and 1-cm in diameter.
3. Shallow fry them in ghee till golden brown and remove them from the pan.
4. Place the rolls in the same frying pan. Fry them till brown. Slice each into two.
5. Sandwich potato rolls, covered with a slice of onion and a slice of tomato, in sliced bun rolls. Hold together with tooth-picks and wrap them in paper napkins. Serve with tomato sauce.

PINEAPPLE SQUASH
ANNANAS KA SHARBAT

Preparation Time : 10 mins.
Cooking Time : 45 mins.

INGREDIENTS

Pineapple juice 4 tea cups	Potassium meta-bi-sulphate $^{1}/_{4}$ tsp
Pineapple essence 1 tsp	Citric acid 5 gm
Sugar 500 gm	Fresh pineapple 1 ½ kg
Water 3 cups	

METHOD

1. Pressure cook the fresh pineapple in water for about 20 minutes.
2. Strain the juice.
3. Mix sugar and citric acid in it and let it simmer on medium fire till they are dissolved.
4. Then boil the syrup till it makes one thread consistency.
5. Add pineapple juice and boil the syrup for 3-4 minutes.
6. Remove from the fire and cool.
7. Add pineapple essence and potassium-meta-bi-sulphate.
8. Cool and pour into sterilized bottles.

Lemon Squash

Neemboo ka Sharbat

Preparation Time : 15 mins.
Cooking Time : 20 mins.

Ingredients

- Lemons 1 kg
- Sugar 1½ kg
- Water 1 pint
- Citric acid 1 tsp or 5 gm
- Potassium meta-bi-sulphate ¼ tsp

Method

1. Take out the juice from the lemons.
2. Prepare the syrup of sugar, water and citric acid.
3. Remove it from the fire. Strain and cool.
4. Add the juice and strain through a muslin cloth.
5. Dissolve potassium-meta-bi-sulphate in a little syrup and mix in.
6. Pour into sterilized bottles when cool.
7. Cork with sterilized tops.

Mixed Fruit Punch

Preparation Time : 15 mins.
Cooking Time : –

Ingredients

Orange juice 8 tbsp
Pineapple juice 8 tbsp
Fresh lemon juice 4 tbsp
Powdered sugar 4 tbsp
Soda water 8 tbsp
Ice-water 8 tbsp

Method

1. Mix lemon juice and orange juice.
2. Then add ice-water and mix sugar in it.
3. Add soda water and pineapple juice.
4. Mix it well.
5. Chill it in the fridge.
6. Serve it in juice glasses. Garnish with a few drops of cream.

ORANGE-SODA

Preparation Time : 10 mins.
Cooking Time : 10 mins.

INGREDIENTS

- Orange essence 3 tsp
- Citric acid 1½ tsp
- Orange colouring 2 tsp
- Sugar 4 cups
- Water 3 cups
- Soda 1 bottle

METHOD

1. Dissolve sugar in water on a slow fire.
2. Add citric acid powder and cook it for a few minutes till it is a sticky syrup.
3. Strain it through a muslin cloth.
4. Add essence and colour.
5. Add the prepared syrup just before serving to cold soda.

Mango Fool

Preparation Time : 25 mins.
Cooking Time

Ingredients

- Puree of ripe mangoes 1 cup
- Cream ¼ cup
- Lemon juice 1 tsp
- Sugar 1 tsp
- Ice-water 2 cups

Method

1. Whip the cream.
2. Mix the whipped cream and lemon juice.
3. Whip the mango puree and add to the cream mixture.
4. Mix sugar in ice-water and add it to the above mixture.
5. Mix it well so that it blends nicely.
6. Put it into glasses, and chill.
7. Serve chilled.

Fruit-Ice

Preparation Time : 20 mins.
Cooking Time : –

Ingredients

Orange juice ½ cup	Sugar, powdered ½ cup
Bananas 2	Lemon juice 3 tbsp
Pineapple juice ½ cup	Cream ½ cup
Milk cooled ½ cup	Soda 1 cup

Method

1. Peel the bananas and place them in a bowl and mash with the lemon juice.
2. Add the pineapple and orange juices.
3. Add the sugar and milk.
4. Mix it well with an egg beater.
5. When the sugar dissolves, add soda and mix it well.
6. Fill juice glasses.
7. Decorate each glass with 2 tbsp of cream.
8. Chill in the fridge. Serve ice-cold.

Morning Dew

Preparation Time : 15 mins.
Cooking Time : –

Ingredients

- Ginger juice ½ cup
- Pineapple juice 1 cup
- Lemon juice ½ tbsp
- Sugar, powdered 2 tbsp

Method

1. Mix ginger juice, pineapple juice, lemon juice and sugar.
2. Chill in the refrigerator and serve it cold in juice glasses.

TOMATO JUICE COCKTAIL

Preparation Time : 15 mins.
Cooking Time : –

Ingredients

Tomato juice 1 cup

Buttermilk 8 tbsp

Lemon juice 1 tbsp

Sugar 2 tbsp

METHOD

1. Mix sugar in tomato juice.
2. Then add buttermilk, and lemon juice to it.
3. Mix well.
4. Chill the tomato-juice cocktail in the fridge.

Note: There should be no grains of butter in the buttermilk.

Chutneys, Sauces and Pickles

India is the home of fragrant spices. The variety of pickles, chutneys and sauces we get here is tremendous. They are a necessary accompaniment to vegetarian food. Chutneys, sauces and pickles enhance the taste of any food. They should be prepared when vegetables are available in abundance. Special care should be taken while preserving them. Bottles should be properly cleaned and sterilized.

Green Mango and Mint Chutney
Aam aur Pudeene ki Chutney

Preparation Time : 20 mins.
Cooking Time : –

Ingredients

Green mango 1 small

Mint 1 bunch

Onion 1 small

Green chillies 2-3

Sugar 1 tbsp

Salt 1 tsp

Method

1. Peel and cut the mango into very small bits.
2. Chop green chillies, onion and mint leaves finely.
3. Grind mango bits, green chillies, mint leaves together.
4. While grinding add salt, sugar and 1 tbsp of water.
5. Continue grinding till it makes a fine paste.
6. Remove from the grinder and put it in a dish.

APPLE CHUTNEY

Preparation Time : 25 mins.
Cooking Time : 30 mins.

INGREDIENTS

Green apples 2 kg
Sugar 750 gm
Vinegar 2 cups
Raisins 250 gm
Ginger 30 gm
Salt to taste

METHOD

1. Peel, core and cut the apples into slices and put them into a pan.
2. Cut the raisins and chop the ginger.
3. Put raisins and ginger in the same pan.
4. Add one cup of water and cook all the ingredients till apples become tender.
5. Add sugar and vinegar and continue to cook till a thick consistency is obtained.
6. Put it into jars while still hot.
7. Cork the jars when the chutney becomes cool.

Mint and Coconut Chutney

Pudeene Aur Nariyal ki Chutney

Preparation Time : 30 mins.
Cooking Time : –

Ingredients

- Coconut 1/4
- Mint 1 small bunch
- Green chillies 2
- Garlic cloves 3-4
- Tamarind pulp 2 tbsp
- Sugar ¼ tsp
- Salt to taste

Method

1. Grind coconut, mint leaves, garlic and green chillies to a fine paste.
2. Then add the tamarind pulp, sugar and salt to taste.
3. Mix it well.

Coriander and Mint Chutney
Dhaniya aur Pudeene ki Chutney

Preparation Time : 20 mins.
Cooking Time : –

Ingredients

- Mint 1 small bunch
- Green coriander 2 small bunches
- Pomegranate seeds 2 tsp
- Sugar 1 tsp
- Green chillies 2
- Onion 1 medium
- Salt ½ tsp

Method

1. Chop onion, mint leaves, coriander leaves and green chillies.
2. Then add pomegranate seeds, sugar and salt.
3. Grind all the ingredients together into a smooth paste.
4. To thin it, add 1-2 tbsp of water.
5. Remove it from the grinder and put it in a dish.

North Indian Mint Chutney
Pudeena Chutney

Preparation Time : 20 mins.
Cooking Time : –

Ingredients

- Mint 1 bunch
- Onion 1 large
- Green chillies 3-4
- Pomegranate seeds 2 tsp
- Sugar 1 tsp
- Salt to taste

Method

1. Wash mint leaves and green chillies. Chop them along with the onion.
2. Then grind all the chopped vegetables and other ingredients into a fine paste.
3. While grinding a little water can be added.
4. Remove from the grinder and put it in a dish.

Curd and Onion Chutney
Dahi aur Pyaz ki Chutney

Preparation Time : 15 mins.
Cooking Time : –

Ingredients

Onions 250 gm

Sour curd 250 gm

Green chillies 10-12

Salt to taste

Method

1. Grate onions, add salt and leave for 5 minutes.
2. Beat curd well.
3. Squeeze the water out of onions.
4. Add chopped green chillies and onions to the curd.
5. Beat it well, and serve.

MIXED FRUIT CHUTNEY
PHALON KI CHUTNEY

Preparation Time : 30 mins.
Cooking Time : 15 mins.

INGREDIENTS

Apples 2 large	Vinegar ½ cup
Peaches 10	Sugar ½ cup
Plums 10	Oil 4 tbsp
Raisins 100 gm	Red chilli powder and salt to taste
Chopped walnuts ½ cup	

METHOD

1. Peel and grate the apples.
2. Discard the stones from peaches and plums and grate them also.
3. Add walnuts, raisins, sugar, vinegar, chilli powder and salt to the grated fruit.
4. Heat oil in a stainless steel pan and add all the ingredients.
5. Cook till concentrated.
6. Serve when cool.

MANGO CHUTNEY
AAM KI CHUTNEY

Preparation Time : 30 mins.
Cooking Time : 30 mins.

INGREDIENTS

- Mangoes 2 kg
- Sugar 1 kg
- Ginger 150 gm
- Garlic 150 gm
- Raisins 250 gm
- Vinegar 1 cup
- Red chilli powder 2 tbsp
- Salt 2 tbsp

METHOD

1. Peel the mangoes and grate them well.
2. Boil them in a pan with sugar and little water till the consistency of jam is acquired.
3. Add chopped ginger, garlic, chilli powder, raisins, vinegar and salt.
4. Cook till all the ingredients are well mixed and it thickens again.
5. Cool and preserve it in sterilized jars.

White Sauce

Preparation Time : 5 mins.
Cooking Time : 10 mins.

Ingredients

- Butter 4 tbsp
- Flour 4 tbsp
- Milk 2 cups
- Pepper ¼ tsp
- Salt 1 tsp

Method

1. Melt butter over low heat, add flour and pepper.
2. Stir until well blended.
3. Remove from the heat, gradually stir in milk and return to heat.
4. Add salt and cook stirring constantly till smooth.
5. Serve hot or cold.

Cheese Sauce

Preparation Time : 5 mins.
Cooking Time : 10 mins.

Ingredients

- White sauce 2 tbsp
- Grated cheese 1 tbsp
- Mustard powder 1 tbsp
- Worcester sauce 1 tbsp

Method

1. Combine mustard powder and Worcester sauce with the white sauce.
2. Stir in the grated cheese.
3. Heat on a slow fire until the cheese melts and mixes in well.
4. Remove it from the fire and serve hot or cold.

Note: This can be used as a sandwitch filling too.

TOMATO KETCHUP
TAMATAR KI SAUCE

Preparation Time : 20 mins.
Cooking Time : 25 mins.

INGREDIENTS

Tomatoes 2 kg	Vinegar ½ cup
Sugar 100 gm	Acetic acid ½ tsp
Cloves 5-6	Water 1 cup
Cinnamon 1-cm piece	Salt 2 tsp
Red chilli powder ½ tsp	

METHOD

1. Chop the tomatoes into small pieces.
2. Add cloves and cinnamon and water.
3. Cook for a few minutes in a stainless steel pan.
4. Strain the juice, add sugar, salt, vinegar and chilli powder.
5. Cook stirring constantly till thick.
6. Remove it from the fire and cool.
7. When absolutely cool, add acetic acid.
8. Stir well to mix. Put this sauce in sterilized bottles and cork.

CHOCOLATE SAUCE

Preparation Time : 15 mins.
Cooking Time : 15 mins.

INGREDIENTS

Chocolate powder 4 tbsp

Cocoa 1 tbsp

Sugar 3 tbsp

Butter 1 tbsp

Cornflour 2 tbsp

Hot water 2 cups

Cold water 3 tbsp

METHOD

1. Mix cocoa and chocolate powder in a little hot water then add two full cups of hot water and mix.
2. Mix cornflour and cold water to form a paste.
3. Stir in cocoa and chocolate mixture.
4. Add sugar.
5. Cook this sauce over boiling water stirring constantly.
6. Continue cooking till the sauce is thick and smooth.
7. Add butter and remove it from the fire.
8. Cool and serve with any pudding or cake.

APPLE SAUCE
SAEB KA SAUCE

Preparation Time : 15 mins.
Cooking Time : 15 mins.

INGREDIENTS

- Apples 2
- Sugar 2 tbsp
- Cloves 3
- Water ½ cup

METHOD

1. Peel, core and chop the apples.
2. Grind the cloves into a powder.
3. Put all the ingredients in a pan.
4. Cook till apples become tender.
5. Blend well so that it forms a fine paste. Serve hot.

Note: Pineapple sauce is also made in the same way but instead of apples, pineapples are used. Pineapple juice is used instead of water.

Indian Sauce
Hindustani Sauce

Preparation Time : 10 mins.
Cooking Time : 15 mins.

Ingredients

- Vinegar ½ cup
- Sugar 1 tbsp
- Raisins 1 tbsp
- Cloves 3
- Grated ginger ½ tsp
- Red chilli powder ½ tsp
- Garlic 5 cloves
- Salt, pepper and cinnamon to taste

Method

1. Grind all the ingredients together except sugar, vinegar and raisins.
2. Put half the sugar into a pan and pour in vinegar.
3. Add remaining sugar.
4. Boil for 5 minutes.
5. Cool and strain.
6. Add the ground ingredients and raisins.
7. Heat it for 5-7 minutes. Then remove from the fire.
8. Serve when cool.

Shredded Mango Pickle
Aam ka Kutra

Preparation Time : 30 mins.
Cooking Time : –

Ingredients

- Raw mangoes 2½ kg
- Mustard oil 250 gm
- Methe 8 tbsp
- Aniseed 6 tbsp
- Onion seeds 2 tbsp
- Turmeric 1 tbsp
- Red chilli powder 2 tbsp
- Black peppercorns 2 tbsp
- Salt 2 tbsp

Method

1. Skin and cut the mangoes into small pieces and remove the kernels.
2. Add turmeric, chilli powder, salt and peppercorns. Mix well.
3. Add methe, aniseeds and onion seeds.
4. Heat oil. Remove, cool and pour over the mangoes.
5. Keep the pickle in the sun for 10 days. Then it is ready for use.

STUFFED MANGO PICKLE
BHARYAN AAM KA ACHAAR

Preparation Time : 1 hr.
Cooking Time : –

INGREDIENTS

Mangoes 2½ kg	Nutmeg powder 1 tbsp
Vinegar 250 ml	Mace powder 1 tbsp
Onion seeds 1 tbsp	Red chilli powder 1 tbsp
Fenugreek seeds 1 tbsp	Black pepper 1 tbsp
Aniseed 1 tbsp	Salt 200 gm
White cardamom powder 1 tbsp	

METHOD

1. Peel the mangoes and slit them in four without severing the ends.
2. Remove the kernels.
3. Mix the spices and add salt.
4. Fill the mixed spices into the mangoes.
5. Tie each mango with a thread to prevent the stuffing from spilling out.
6. Put into a jar and keep it in the sun for 10 days.
7. Shake the jar every day.

NORTH INDIAN MANGO PICKLE
AAM KA ACHAAR

Preparation Time : 1 hr.
Cooking Time : –

INGREDINENTS

Mangoes 5 kg	
Red chilli powdar 100 gm	
Fenugreek seeds 50 gm	
Aniseed 75 gm	
Mustard oil 700 gm	
Turmeric 30 gm	
Salt 700 gm	

METHOD

1. Cut the mangoes into pieces.
2. In a flat dish, mix all the spices and mangoes with little musturd oil.
3. Put in the jars and add the rest of the oil to cover the mangoes.
4. Keep in the sun for a few days.
5. Shake it daily so that the oil comes to the top.
6. Use the pickle when the mangoes are soft.

SWEET AND SOUR CHILLI PICKLE
KHAT-MEETHA MIRCH KA ACHAAR

Preparation Time : Overnight
Cooking Time : 30 mins.

INGREDINENTS

Green chillies 1 kg	Garlic 1 pod
Sugar 1 sup	Cumin seeds 1 tbsp
Vinger 3 cups	Oli 500 gm
Turmeric powder 1 tbsp	Tamarind 200 gm
Musturd seeds 25 gm	Salt to taste
Ginger 50 gm	

METHOD

1. Grind ginger and garlic
2. Soak tamarind in vinegar overnight.
3. Wash chillies and drain. Cut off their heads and slit them.
4. Strain the tamarind pulp in the vinegar and mix sugar in it.
5. Heat oil and fry garlic-ginger paste till brown.
6. Now add all the masalas, turmeric, mustard powdar and cumin seeds. Fry a little.
7. Put in the green chillies and fry till the colour changes.
8. Now add the tamarind pulp and sugar and cook for 5 minutes more. Take it off the fire and add salt to taste. Its ready to be served when cool.

Sweet Lime Pickle I
Neemboo ka Achaar

Preparation Time : 30 mins.
Cooking Time : 15 mins.

Ingredients

- Limes ½ kg
- Sugar 250 gm
- Red chilli powder 5 tsp
- Turmeric powder 2 tsp
- Asafoetida 1 tsp
- Salt 6 tbsp

Method

1. Cut each lime into half, extract half the juice of the limes.
2. Steam the limes till they become soft.
3. Mix the remaining ingredients and stuff into the limes.
5. Add the lime juice and mix thoroughly.
6. Put in a jar and keep it in the sun for 2-3 days.

Sweet Lime Pickle II

Neemboo ka Achaar

Preparation Time : 30mins.
Cooking Time : –

Ingredients

Sour limes 24	Aniseed 50 gm
Sugar 1 kg	Red chilli powder 30 gm
Turmeric powder 50 gm	Asafoetida 5 gm
Split mustard seeds 50 gm	Split fenugreek seeds 100 gm
Split coriander seeds 50 gm	Salt 50 gm

Method

1. Wash the sour limes and slit into four parts.
2. Mix salt and turmeric powder. Add to limes and put them into a jar.
3. Stir every day for 10 days.
4. Take the limes out and put them in the shade to dry for 3-4 hours.
5. Mix the rest of the ingredients well and add to the lime pieces.
6. Store in a glass jar, keep it for about 15 days.

STUFFED LIMES
BHARVAN NEEMBOO

Preparation Time : 40 mins.
Cooking Time : 5 mins.

INGREDIENTS

Limes 25	Fenugreek seeds 25 gm
Red chillies 25 gm	Mustard seeds 25 gm
Garlic 30 gm	Turmeric pieces 10 gm
Mustard seeds 30 gm	Oil 4 tbsp
Vinegar 2 tbsp	Salt 250 gm

METHOD

1. Slit the limes into four without slicing right through.
2. Fry the turmeric pieces in some oil and grind them in vinegar.
3. Grind the red chillies, garlic, mustard and fenugreek seeds separately.
4. Then mix them with turmeric paste and salt. Stuff this mixture into the limes.
5. Add oil and put them in a jar and store for 2-3 days. Then put the jar in the sun for 2 days.

Carrot Pickle
Gajar ka Achaar

Preparation Time : 30 mins.
Cooking Time 5 mins.

Ingredients

- Carrots 250 gm
- Oil 1 tbsp
- Sour lime juice to taste
- Asafoetida 1 pinch
- Red chilli powder 25 gm
- Mustard powder 25 gm
- Turmeric powder ½ tsp
- Salt 25 gm

Method

1. Wash the carrots and cut them into 5-cm pieces.
2. Add salt, chilli, turmeric and mustard powder and mix thoroughly.
3. Heat the oil and brown the asafoetida, remove from the fire.
4. When cool, add to carrots along with sour lime juice and store in glass jars.

Cauliflower & Turnip Pickle
Gobhi-Shalgam ka Achaar

Ingredients

Cauliflower 3 kg	Red chilli powder 150 gm
Turnips 2½ kg	Cumin seeds 10 gm
Mustard oil $^{3}/_{4}$ kg	Cardamom 8 gm
Vinegar 750 ml	Cloves 10 gm
Ginger 5 cm piece	Mustard seeds 100 gm
Onions 150 gm	Salt 300 gm
Cinnamon 5-cm piece	

Method

1. Peel the turnips.
2. Cut the cauliflower and turnips into pieces.
3. Chop the onions.
4. Wash, drain and spread the vegetables in the sun for two hours to dry.
5. Grind all the spices except mustard seeds into a fine paste and brown them in oil.
6. Then add onions, cauliflower and turnips and salt.
7. Add mustard seeds last of all and stir fry. After 3-4 minutes remove it from the fire.
8. When cool, put it in the jars, close the lids and keep in the sun for 2-3 days.
9. Then add vinegar and keep it in the sun for 2-3 days more.

GLOSSARY

English	Hindi
Almonds	Badaam
Alum	Phitkar
Aniseeds	Saunf
Asafoetida	Hing
Bay leaf	Tejpatta
Black gram	Urad dal
Brinjal	Baingan
Capsicum	Simla mirch
Cardamom (black)	Badi elaichi
Cardamom (green)	Chhoti elaichi
Cashewnuts	Kaju
Cinnamon	Dalchini
Citric acid	Nimboo ka Sat
Cloves	Laung
Coriander leaves	Hara dhania
Coriander powder	Pissa dhania
Coriander seeds	Sabut dhania
Cumin seeds	Jeera
Dates	Khajoor
Fenugreek leaves	Hari methi
Fenugreek seeds	Methe
Garlic	Lasun
Gingelly/ sesame seeds	Til
Ginger	Adrak
Gram flour	Besan
Jaggery	Gur
Lime	Nimbu
Mango powder	Amchoor
Marrow	Ghia
Mint leaves	Hara pudina
Mustard seeds (black)	Sarson
Mustard seeds (brown)	Rai
Nutmeg	Jaiphal
Peppercorns	Sabutkalimirch
Pomegranate seeds	Anardana
Pumpkin	Petha
Raisins	Kishmish
Saffron	Kesar
Semolina	Sooji (rawa)
Spinach	Palak
Sweet potato	Shakarkandi
Tamarind	Imli
Turmeric	Haldi
Vinegar	Sirka
Walnuts	Akhroat
White Bengal gram	Kabuli chana